Mathew Price

# THE CHRISTMAS STOCKINGS

*Illustrated by*
Errol Le Cain

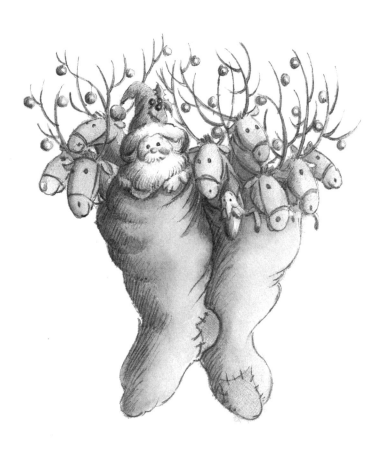

BARRON'S
New York

It's Christmas Eve.
Santa has come to fill
two little stockings with toys
– but there's no chimney.
How will he get down?
Can *you* help him?

*To Dalton,*
*"Merry Christmas!"*
*Love,*
*Uncle Mike, Aunt Dwaj & Messi*
*1992*

First edition for the United States
published 1987 by
Barron's Educational Series, Inc.

Designed and produced by Mathew Price Ltd
Kingston upon Thames, Surrey, England

Text © Mathew Price 1987
Illustrations © Errol Le Cain 1987

All inquiries should be addressed to:
Barron's Educational Series, Inc.
250 Wireless Boulevard
Hauppauge, NY 11788

Library of Congress Catalog Card No. 87-12444

International Standard Book No. 0-8120-5870-4

**Library of Congress Cataloging-in-Publication Data**

Price, Mathew.
    The Christmas stockings.

    Summary: On Christmas Eve Santa goes slightly astray
in a large apartment building before finally finding the
stockings he seeks to fill.
    1. Santa Claus – Juvenile fiction.    [1. Santa Claus –
Fiction.    2. Christmas – Fiction.    3. Apartment houses –
Fiction]    I. Le Cain, Errol, ill.    II. Title.
PZ7.P93135Ch 1987      [E]      87-12444
ISBN 0-8120-5870-4

Printed in Hong Kong

9   8   7   6   5   4   3   2   1

Well, he's inside the house, but there are no stockings here. Where can he go now?

Still no stockings
– we'll have to help him again.
Can you find another door?

A Christmas party! What fun!
But we can't stop here.
We've got to find those stockings.
Where's the way out?

There they are!